The Kids of the
Polk Street School
9

PURPLE CLIMBING DAYS

DAYS

Patricia Reilly Giff

Illustrated by Blanche Sims

A YEARLING BOOK

Published by
Bantam Doubleday Dell Books for Young Readers
a division of
Bantam Doubleday Dell Publishing Group, Inc.
1540 Broadway
New York, New York 10036

ISBN: 0-440-47309-8

Printed in the United States of America

May 1985

26

CW

To Helene Steinhauer

Chapter 1

Richard Best rushed down the hall.

He couldn't wait to get in the classroom.

"Faster," he said to his friend Emily Arrow.

They started to run.

"No running," shouted the sixth-grade monitor.

They slowed down a little.

They turned the corner.

They burst into Room 113.

Today was skink day.

Everyone was in the classroom ahead of them.

1

All the kids.

Ms. Rooney.

Mrs. Stewart, the student teacher, who used to be Ms. Vincent.

Matthew Jackson poked Richard on the arm. "Hey, Beast," he said. "It's going to be a great day."

Richard nodded. Skink day, he thought.

"Climbing day," said Matthew.

Richard closed his eyes for a second.

Climbing day.

He had forgotten all about it.

He was supposed to climb the rope in gym.

Climb it to the top.

He didn't even like to climb the monkey bars.

"Today I'm going to grab that rope . . ." Matthew began. "Today I'm going right up there."

Richard put his books in his desk.

Today was the day he was going to fall off the gym ceiling. He was going to break his neck.

"Look, Beast," Matthew said. He jumped on his chair.

He stretched his arms over his head.

He made believe he was holding the rope.

He raised one foot in the air. "Right to the top. . . ."

Ms. Rooney looked up from her desk. "Matthew Jackson," she said. "It's too early in the morning to start."

Matthew jumped off his chair. "See what I mean?" he told Richard. "That's the way I'm going to climb."

Richard didn't answer.

He thought about the fat brown rope.

The fat brown rope with the fat brown knots.

It was hanging down from the gym ceiling.

He felt dizzy just thinking about it.

He rubbed his hands on his jeans.

Think of the skink, he told himself.

He looked back at the science table.

Wayne was supposed to bring in the skink tank. He said he had one at home.

The only tank on the table was the fish tank.

"Hey," Richard said. "Where's the skink tank?"

Matthew raised his shoulders in the air.

"How can we have a skink if we don't have a skink tank?" Richard asked.

"Don't worry," Wayne said from his seat. "It'll be here on time."

"Last call for lunch money," Ms. Rooney said.

Richard poked his head in his desk.

No lunch.

No lunch money either.

He went to the front of the room. "I forgot my—"

"That's no way to start the week," said Ms. Rooney. She reached into her purse. "Pay me back tomorrow."

Richard nodded. "What time is the skink coming?" he asked.

5

Ms. Rooney put a check next to his name. "Chocolate milk or white?"

"Chocolate," he said. "What time is—"

Ms. Rooney looked up. "This is Monday."

"Right," said Richard.

"You forgot," said Ms. Rooney. "Wednesday is skink day."

Richard went back to his seat.

Monday.

Some kind of chopped-up stuff for lunch.

And no skink.

Matthew was standing next to his desk. He was making circles in the air with his foot. "I'm warming up," he said. "For the climbing."

Richard swallowed.

"Line up," said Ms. Rooney. "Time for gym."

Slowly Richard went to the front of the room.

He wished he could hide somewhere until gym was over.

Chapter 2

The class went down the hall.

At the front of the line Ms. Rooney stopped.

Mrs. Kara was working on a bulletin board.

Pink letters marched along the top.

MOTHER'S DAY IS COMING

"Looks great," said Ms. Rooney.

Mrs. Kara sighed. "Blue Monday," she said. "I need a longer weekend."

Ms. Rooney nodded. "I know what you mean."

Blue Monday, Richard told himself.

It was worse than blue Monday.

It was purple Monday.

Ms. Rooney turned around. "This is a snake line," she said.

The class straightened the line.

Richard tried to keep his head in back of Matthew's ears.

They started to move again.

Richard passed the bulletin board.

Mrs. Kara was putting a row of tulips along the bottom.

They looked like kindergarten flowers.

Baby flowers.

He flicked his finger at one of the stems.

"If you don't mind," Mrs. Kara said.

He ducked his head and kept going.

The class marched into the gym.

Richard looked up.

The ceiling was high.

Almost high enough for an airplane.

He looked down.

He didn't want to see the rope.

"Have a good time," Ms. Rooney said.

She went out to the hall again.

Richard looked around.

He wondered where Mr. Bell, the gym teacher, was.

"Snaggle doodles," yelled Emily. "The rope."

Emily grabbed the rope. "I can do it with my eyes closed," she said. "I can almost do it with one hand."

"Go, Emily," yelled Matthew. "I'm right behind you."

Emily started up the rope.

Richard closed his eyes.

"Hurry," yelled Matthew. "I'm next."

Just then the door opened.

It was Mrs. Miller, the meanest substitute teacher in the school.

She was wearing blue shorts and a blue sweatshirt.

She looked like a big blue hippopotamus.

A blue hippopotamus with little skinny legs and black sneakers.

"I can swing like Tarzan," Emily yelled.

Mrs. Miller looked up.

She blew her whistle. "Get down here this minute," she shouted.

Emily started down.

"Who told you to climb?" Mrs. Miller said. "And without a gym teacher here to watch you."

Emily jumped off the rope. "I'm tough," she said. "I won't fall."

"I don't want to hear another word," said Mrs. Miller. She turned to the class. "Today I'm Mr. Bell."

Everyone laughed a little.

Richard raised his hand quickly. "I can't do climbing today."

He crossed his fingers. "My mother said."

Mrs. Miller stared at him.

"I want to climb," he said.

He crossed his fingers in back of him. "I'm dying to climb. Right to the top."

Mrs. Miller was still looking at him.

"My mother said I can't." Richard shook his head. He tried to look sad.

Mrs. Miller frowned. "We're not climbing ropes today," she said. "We're going to play 'A tisket, a tasket, a green and yellow basket.' "

Everybody made a groaning sound.

Richard took a deep breath.

He was saved.

"It was my favorite game when I was young," said Mrs. Miller.

"That's a baby game," Emily said under her breath. "It's for kindergarten kids."

Mrs. Miller blew her whistle. "You're not playing anything," she told Emily. "Sit on the bleachers."

"Too bad we can't climb," Richard told Matthew.

Matthew looked as if he wanted to cry. "I was waiting to climb all weekend," he said.

"It's probably your fault, Beast," said Jason Bazyk. "All that stuff about your mother."

"Maybe Mr. Bell will be back soon," Richard said. "Maybe he just has a cold."

He waved his hand in the air.

"Yes?" Mrs. Miller asked.

"Did Mr. Bell break his leg?" he asked.

Richard tried to cross his toes in his sneakers.

Then he uncrossed them. It wasn't nice to wish Mr. Bell had broken his leg.

"Of course not," Mrs. Miller said.

Richard watched Emily go over to the bleachers.

On the way she grabbed the rope.

She looked back at Mrs. Miller.

Emily had her worst mad face, Richard thought.

13

Emily was much tougher than he was.

Jason came over to him. "This is all you fault," he said. "And your mother's too."

"What's the matter with your mother any way?" Timothy Barbiero asked.

"Nothing," Richard said.

He thought about his mother.

His mother didn't know they were going to climb.

She probably would have been glad.

She probably would have said, "That's great."

Richard shook his head.

They started to play 'A tisket, a tasket.'

Nobody even called on him.

Chapter 3

It was Wednesday.

Skink day, at last.

Beast and Emily went down the hall.

On the way to their class they passed the gym.

Richard opened the door a tiny bit.

They peeked inside.

Mrs. Miller was in front of the bleachers.

She was jumping up and down on her little skinny legs.

"Snaggle doodles," said Emily. "No climbing again."

She made a face.

Richard tried to make a mad face too.

"I'm going to tell Ms. Rooney," said Emily. "Or even Mr. Mancina. Mr. Bell wants us to climb."

Richard swallowed. "Maybe you'd better not."

"Hey," said Emily. "Here comes Wayne."

Wayne was carrying a big fish tank.

Next to him was Matthew Jackson.

Matthew was carrying his own books under one arm. He had Wayne's under the other.

He was holding two paper bag lunches with his teeth.

Richard could see the tops of the lunch bags were wet from Matthew's mouth.

He wondered if Wayne minded.

They marched into the classroom.

Richard tapped Emily on the shoulder.

He had to tell her not to ask about climbing.

He'd say . . .

What could he say?

Maybe he could say his mother would be mad.

But everyone was rushing back to the science table.

Richard rushed back too.

He grabbed a spot next to the tank.

He stood right next to Emily.

"Listen, Emily," he began. "You'd better not—"

The door opened.

It was Mr. Mancina, the principal. He had a brown box in his hands.

"It's the skink," said Emily. "Finally. We have a class pet."

"We've had fish all along," Wayne said.

"That doesn't count," Emily said. "Everyone has fish. A skink is better."

Everyone crowded around the table.

18

Richard held on to the edge. He didn't want anyone to push him out of the way.

"Don't tell—" he began.

Mr. Mancina came to the back of the room. "Excuse me," he said to Richard.

Richard had to move over.

He tried to squeeze between Timothy and Matthew.

Matthew had wet the bed last night.

Richard held his fingers over his nose. He tried to breathe from his mouth.

At the same time he tried to get Emily's attention.

Matthew looked at Richard.

Richard made believe he was scratching his nose.

Mr. Mancina put the box into the tank.

Then he opened the top of the box.

Everyone leaned over.

"Psst," Richard said to Emily.

"He's down at the bottom of the box," Matthew said. "I can see some brownish—"

"Grayish—" said Jason.

"Here he comes," said Matthew.

"He looks like a dinosaur," said Jill Simon.

"He's a lizard," said Ms. Rooney. "That means he's related to a snake."

"I don't like snakes," said Jill. "That means I might not like a skink."

"He's cold-blooded like a snake," Ms. Rooney said. "His body stays about as warm or cold as the air he's in."

Richard gave Emily a little kick under the table.

"Ouch," Emily said.

"Careful," said Mr. Mancina.

"He's a big one," Wayne said. "Longer than my pencil."

"Maybe he's hungry," said Timothy.

"We could give him some of Drake and Harry's fish food," Emily said.

Mr. Mancina shook his head. "He eats crickets."

"Yuck," Jill said.

"He thinks they're delicious," Mr. Mancina said.

He reached into his pocket.

He pulled out a small white box.

"Here," he told Jill. "Take these."

Jill reached out. "What . . ."

"Skink dinner," said Mr. Mancina. "Crickets."

"Yeow," said Jill.

She backed away from the table.

Mr. Mancina dropped the box.

"You're standing on my foot," Matthew told Jill. "I'm caving in."

The black crickets scattered across the table.

Four people screamed.

Richard opened his mouth. "Emily," he said without making any noise.

Emily scooped up a cricket. "What?"

"The climbing," he said. "Don't—"

"Right," said Emily.

"Look at that guy go," Matthew yelled.

21

Emily tapped Mr. Mancina on the arm. "How come we can't climb?"

"Climb?"

Richard leaned over the tank. He held his breath. The skink was looking at him.

"In the gym," Emily said. "Mr. Bell is absent. Now Mrs. Miller won't let us climb."

Mr. Mancina started for the door. He winked at them. "Better give a lesson on cricket catching," he told Ms. Rooney.

Then he went out to the hall.

Jill started to cry. "I'm not sitting in here," she said. "Suppose I sit on a cricket?"

"He'll be squished," said Timothy.

"Flatter than a pancake," Jason said.

"Flatter than a potato chip," said Wayne.

"That's enough," Ms. Rooney said.

"Maybe we'll get to climb tomorrow," said Emily.

"Great," Matthew said. He gave Richard a little punch.

"Great," said Richard.

The skink opened its mouth. Its tongue darted back and forth at Richard.

Richard darted his tongue back and forth too.

"He's a brave guy, that skink," said Jason.

"Right," Richard said.

The skink was still looking at him.

Richard wondered if the skink knew he was afraid.

He hoped not.

He stepped back from the tank.

The skink was still staring at him.

Richard sighed.

The skink knew. He was sure of it.

Chapter 4

It was after school.

Richard was alone in the classroom.

He could hear a cricket chirping.

It must have been in someone's desk.

Richard was board monitor for May.

It was a great job.

The greatest.

He sloshed water over the board.

The water ran down in dark lines.

Then he ran along next to the ledge.

He raced the sponge along the ledge too.

He was probably the fastest board monitor in the world.

He looked at the erasers.

They were full of chalk.

He was supposed to take them outside.

He had to clap them near the gym doors.

But Jason and Matthew and Timothy were in the gym. Climbing.

Instead Richard clapped the erasers in the air.

The dust made him cough.

He went over to the skink tank.

Only the skink's head was showing.

The rest of it was buried under the sawdust stuff at the bottom.

The skink looked up at him.

Richard made a friendly face at it.

He tried to look as brave as he could.

"Hey, Rocky," he said.

The skink didn't move.

"Hey, Spiderman."

"What are you doing?" Jim the custodian asked. He was standing at the door.

"Trying to find a skink name," Beast said. "A brave one. What do you think of Mr. T?"

Jim sprinkled green sawdust on the floor. "Sounds all right to me."

Beast stared at the skink.

The skink was staring back.

"I'm not sure he likes it," Beast said.

"Listen," Jim said. "How about taking the erasers outside? Clean them up a little."

"You don't think they look clean?" Beast asked.

Jim began to sweep. "They look like a mess."

"Well," said Beast. He tapped on the tank. "I think it's getting late."

"Aren't you Ms. Rooney's board monitor?" Jim asked.

Richard nodded a little.

"Got to do your best," Jim said.

Richard sighed. "I guess so."

He picked up the erasers.

Slowly he went downstairs.

He clapped an eraser on the stairway wall.

It left a square white mark.

He made two more marks.

They looked like an *F*.

F for ferocious. Ferocious Freddie the skink.

"Young man," a voice said.

It was Mrs. Kettle, the sixth-grade teacher.

She was a tough one.

Almost as tough as Mrs. Miller.

"Did you make those chalk marks?"

Richard rubbed at them with his sleeve.

Mrs. Kettle came down the stairs.

"When I come up again," she said, "these marks had better be gone."

She turned the corner.

Richard spit on his fingers.

He rubbed the wall a little.

27

Then he stood back.

Not bad.

He raced down the stairs.

He looked in the gym window.

Matthew was climbing up the rope.

He ducked past.

He opened the back door and went outside.

He clapped the two erasers thirty-three times.

There was dust all over the place.

Then he went back inside.

Jason was standing at the door. "Hey, Beast," he said. "Come on in here."

Beast shook his head. "Can't."

"Matthew's almost to the top," Jason said. "He's climbing like a monkey."

Richard waved the erasers around. "Jim's waiting for these."

"Just take a quick look," Jason said.

Richard took a step into the gym.

Matthew was hanging on the rope.

He was halfway to the ceiling.

The rope was swinging back and forth.

Richard closed his eyes.

"What's the matter?" Jason asked.

Matthew started to shimmy down.

Richard opened his eyes. "Nothing."

"You're not afraid?" Jason asked.

"Nuh uh," Richard said. "Not a bit."

"How come your mother said you can't climb he rope?"

"Uh . . ." Richard began.

"You're afraid," said Jason.

"Am not," Richard said.

Matthew jumped down the last foot.

He came over to them. "Great stuff," he said. 'Excellent."

"Give it a try," Jason told Richard.

Richard shook his head. "My mother said . . ." He tried to think. "My mother said I have a trick knee."

29

"What's that?" Matthew said.

Richard tried to remember. He had heard his mother say that his Uncle Pete had one.

"I never heard of a trick knee," said Jason.

"We all have it in my family," Richard said. "My Uncle Pete. My father. Holly. . . ."

"Wow," Matthew said. "What's it look like?"

"Well," Richard began. "When you climb it blows up, sort of. It's dangerous."

Just then Mrs. Kettle stuck her head in the door.

"What are you doing in here? Climbing ropes? Without a teacher?" Mrs. Kettle shook her head. "Dangerous. Very dangerous. Out of the gym. This minute."

Then she looked at Richard. "Did you clean those marks?"

"Yes," Richard said. He edged toward the door.

Mrs. Kettle went down the hall.

"I'm not afraid of danger," Richard said. "But I promised my mother."

He hurried out the back door.

Halfway home he saw he was still carrying the erasers.

Then he remembered. His sister, Holly, was waiting in front of school for him.

He hoped Jason and Matthew didn't ask her about her trick knee.

Chapter 5

It was a rainy day.

Richard walked into the kitchen.

"I don't need boots," Richard told his mother.

"He does so," said Holly. "He's always walking in puddles."

"I do not," Richard said. He opened the cabinet door.

"I'll drive you," his mother said. "What are you doing there?"

"I need a potato," he said. "I'm the potato person today."

"You're a potato head," said Holly. "Every day."

"Want a potato in the face?" Richard asked. He raised his arm.

His mother grabbed his wrist. "Why a potato?"

"It's for the skink," Richard said.

He made a face at Holly. "He needs it. We cut it up. Then he can lick it. It's wet."

"What about water?"

"He gets that too. This is extra."

He stuck the potato in his raincoat pocket.

He picked up his books and started for the driveway.

He watched Holly over his shoulder.

She ran to get ahead of him.

She always wanted to sit in the front.

At the last minute he dived for the car.

He beat her there by half a second.

"It's not fair," Holly told his mother. "He always gets to sit in the front."

"Your turn next time," his mother said. She pulled out of the driveway.

Richard watched the rain against the window. "What's a trick knee?" he asked.

His mother raised her shoulders. "Uncle Pete has one. It's nothing much."

"Jason asked me about that yesterday," Holly said.

Richard turned around. "What did you say?"

"I told him to get lost. He's as crazy as you are."

Richard swallowed.

There was only one thing to do.

Climb the rope.

He had to do it.

Right now.

Before everyone else got to school.

He was going to race up that rope.

Right up to the gym ceiling.

Faster than Matthew.

Faster even than Mr. Bell.

Then he wouldn't be afraid anymore.

He tried to swallow. His mouth was dry.

"Do it," he said under his breath.

"Richard's talking to himself," Holly told his mother.

"That's all right," his mother said. "I talk to myself, too, sometimes."

"Really?" Richard said.

"Really," his mother said. She pulled up in front of school.

Richard opened the car door. He dashed up the path.

He made sure to jump over the puddles.

Then he turned to wave at his mother.

He went straight to the gym.

No one else was there yet.

He dropped his yellow raincoat on the floor.

He put his books on top of it.

Then he went over to the rope.

It had a bunch of fat knots. They went all the way to the top.

"Just grab the first knot," he said aloud.

His voice sounded strange in the empty gym.

He jumped up a little and held on.

The rope began to sway.

He held on tight.

"Nothing to it," he said. He touched the floor with one foot.

The rope stopped moving.

Now the next knot.

He'd really have to get off the floor.

He looked up.

He put one hand up a little higher.

He took his foot off the floor.

The rope started to wiggle.

"Don't pay attention," he said.

He tried to move the other hand.

Suppose he got up high?

Suppose he fell?

Fell on his head?

Broke his leg?

Broke his arm?

Had to get stitches like Drake Evans did last year?

No good.

He put his feet on the floor again.

Just then the door opened.

It was Jason and Timothy Barbiero.

"What are you doing in here?" Jason said.

"I was climbing the rope," said Richard.

"You didn't get very far," Timothy said.

"No," Richard said.

"I thought you had a trick knee or something," Jason said.

"It's all better," Richard said.

"Then climb the rope," said Jason.

"Can't right now," Richard said.

He walked across the gym.

He picked up his books and his raincoat.

"Scared," he heard Jason whisper.

Richard banged out the gym door. He went down the hall to his classroom.

Chapter 6

It was still pouring out.

No outside recess after lunch.

Most of the class was in the auditorium.

They were watching cartoons.

The same ones as last week.

Richard went for a drink of water.

He darted his tongue in and out.

The water dripped down his chin.

He was glad he wasn't a skink.

He went into the classroom.

He stopped to look at the skink.

"Hey, Superman," he said.

The skink blinked its eyes.

"Don't like that name?" Richard asked. "It's a brave one."

He went to his seat.

He tore a piece of paper out of his notebook.

He drew a grayish-brown skink head.

What about skink ears?

He went back to the tank to look.

There was a little hole on each side of the skink's head.

Just then the door opened.

It was Timothy and Jason.

They stopped to look at Richard's drawing. "Great skink," Timothy said.

They went back to the skink tank.

"I wish he'd get out from under the sawdust," Jason said.

42

"Maybe I could . . ." Timothy put his hand into the tank.

The skink moved its head.

Timothy jumped back.

"Afraid?" Jason asked.

"No." Timothy shook his head.

"Richard's afraid too," said Jason.

"I am not," Richard said.

"Sure you are." Jason laughed a little. "You and your mother and your trick knee."

"I told you my trick knee was better," Richard said.

"You never had one," said Jason. "You're scared of the rope."

Richard shook his head. "I'm not scared of anything."

He put his hand into the tank.

Quickly he touched the top of the skink's head.

Surprised, he pulled his hand back. "He feels rough."

"You're afraid," said Jason.

"No," Richard said. "I thought he'd feel smooth and maybe a little wet."

He reached into the tank again.

The skink darted under the sawdust.

Richard poked his finger underneath.

He tried to grab the skink.

The skink darted to the other side of the tank.

"Keep going, Beast," said Jason. "You almost have him."

Richard reached in with both hands.

The skink darted around the tank.

Richard felt a lump in his throat. He knew the skink was afraid. "I'd better stop," he said.

" 'Fraidy cat," Jason said.

Richard closed his fingers around the skink.

He held the skink up by the tail.

Jason and Timothy moved closer.

Richard could feel the skink pulling to get away.

It was pulling as hard as it could.

Richard felt tears in his eyes.

The skink jerked sideways.

"Hey," Jason said.

The skink fell back into the tank.

There was something left in Richard's hands.

Dry. Grayish brown.

"Look what you did," Wayne said.

"It's his tail," Richard said. He knew his voice sounded strange. "He jumped so hard his tail broke off."

He looked down at the skink. He could see him digging into the sawdust.

Where the tail had been was a small drop of blood.

Richard dropped the tail on the science table.

He raced out of the room.

He wondered if the skink was going to die.

Chapter 7

Head down, Richard took the steps two at a time.

He ran right into Mrs. Miller.

"Oof."

He tried to catch his breath.

"What's your name, young man?" Mrs. Miller asked.

"Sorry," Richard said. "It's Rich—"

"No, don't tell me." Mrs. Miller raised her hand in the air. "I know. You're the one with that awful nickname. Beast."

Richard nodded.

"You're the one from that class. The climbing class. The children who want to kill themselves."

"Right."

"Such silliness. Climbing up to the gym ceiling . . ."

"Not me," said Richard.

"Yes, you."

Richard shook his head.

Mrs. Miller stopped talking for a moment. She rubbed her stomach. "Ran right into me," she said. "I can't believe it."

"Sorry," Richard said again.

"You're just the one who's going to fall off the gym ceiling."

Richard didn't answer.

"Break your neck."

"That's what I'm afraid of," Richard said.

"Afraid?" Mrs. Miller asked. "Afraid?"

"Afraid," Richard said. It felt good to say i aloud.

Mrs. Miller took off her eyeglasses.

She rubbed them against her blue sweatshirt.

"Let's get off the stairs," she said. "Nex thing someone else will try to kill me."

She clunked down the stairs.

Richard thought about the skink.

The skink without his tail.

The skink with a little dot of blood.

He followed Mrs. Miller down the stairs.

"I think I killed the class skink," he said.

"Killed a skink?" Mrs. Miller said. "Wha next?"

"I didn't do it on purpose. It was an accident."

Then he shook his head. "I shouldn't hav done it."

"Tail fell off?" Mrs. Miller asked.

Richard nodded.

"Holding him up in the air?"

"Yes."

"Not a very nice thing to do to a skink."

"I know," Richard said.

"Don't worry, though," Mrs. Miller said. "It'll grow a new one."

Richard blinked. "You think so?"

"I know so. Skinks drop their tails off to get away from something." She frowned. "Or someone."

"Oh," Richard said.

"It was afraid, you know," Mrs. Miller said.

"He isn't a coward" Richard said.

Mrs. Miller frowned again. "Being afraid doesn't make you a coward. Everyone's afraid sometimes."

Richard looked at her. He wondered if that were true.

Then he heard the bell ring.

"Time to go back to your room," Mrs. Miller said.

Richard started up the stairs.

51

"It'll grow a new tail," Mrs. Miller called. "I
a little while."

"That's good."

"Young man," Mrs. Miller called again. "An
mal."

Richard turned around. "Beast," he said.

"You're afraid?"

"The gym rope."

Mrs. Miller frowned for the third time.

"See me after school," she said. "In the gym.

Richard hurried toward the classroom.

He couldn't wait to tell everyone.

He couldn't wait to say the skink would grow
new tail.

He stopped at the classroom door.

Miller the Killer.

He wondered what she'd do to him after schoo
Then he started to think.

Mrs. Miller said everyone was afraid sometimes
Everyone?

He couldn't believe it.

Then he thought of Jason and Timothy.

They hadn't touched the skink.

Why not?

Maybe they were afraid.

He bet they were.

He opened the door.

Just then Jill came dashing out. "Save me," she yelled. "There's a cricket in my desk."

"Don't worry," he said.

Inside he could hear Jason laughing.

He could hear Timothy making little chirping noises.

"Skink's going to get you," he yelled at them.

He opened the door.

"Rope's going to get you," Jason yelled back.

Richard swallowed.

They were probably right.

Chapter 8

Richard poked his head out the school door.

"Go home without me," he told his sister Holly.

"Are you in trouble?" Holly asked. "Again?"

Richard didn't answer.

Holly shook her frizzy head. "Mommy's going to be mad."

"Just get out of here," Richard said.

He banged the door shut.

He walked down the hall to the gym.

Mrs. Miller was standing inside. "There you are," she said.

"Yes," Richard said.

For a moment Mrs. Miller didn't say anything.

"Sorry I ran into you," he said.

Mrs. Miller nodded.

"My sister Holly is waiting," Richard said. "I'd better go home now."

Mrs. Miller shook her head. "Don't be silly. We have some business to take care of."

"Oh," Richard said.

"Do you know what everyone calls me?" Mrs. Miller said.

"Uh . . ." Richard said. He looked up at the ceiling. He made believe he was thinking.

"Miller the Killer," said Mrs. Miller.

"Oh," Richard said again.

"Didn't you ever hear that?"

Richard didn't know what to say. "I guess . . . Maybe . . ."

Mrs. Miller leaned forward.

Richard could see the frown lines on her face.

"I'll tell you something," said Mrs. Miller. "There's one way to stop being afraid."

"Really?" Richard asked.

"Climb the rope," said Mrs. Miller.

Richard backed away. "I don't think I . . ."

"That's how you stop being afraid. That's what we're going to do right now."

Mrs. Miller took a step forward. "Guess what?"

"What?"

"I'm afraid of the rope too."

"Really?" Richard asked.

Mrs. Miller grinned. "If I had a tail it would drop off. As soon as I climbed the rope."

Richard started to laugh.

He kept thinking of Mrs. Miller with a tail.

He thought of himself with a tail.

Just then Holly poked her head in the gym.

"Yes?" Mrs. Miller asked.

"I'm waiting for my brother."

Mrs. Miller waved her hand. "Tell your mother that Animal will be home late today."

Holly started to giggle a little.

"Go ahead," Mrs. Miller said.

"Richard's not allowed to cross Linden Avenue," Holly said.

Mrs. Miller put her hands on her hips. "Don't be silly."

"He doesn't look both ways," Holly said.

"I do so," said Richard.

"He certainly will look both ways," said Mrs. Miller. "He's almost out of Ms. Rooney's class. Tell your mother I said so."

Holly closed the gym door.

Inside it was very quiet.

"Now," said Mrs. Miller. "We're going to climb the rope."

Richard rubbed his hands on his jeans. "I tried that," he said. "It didn't work."

"That's because Miller the Killer wasn't around," she said. "I'll catch you if you fall."

Richard ducked his head.

He tried to swallow.

His mouth was dry.

"Grab that rope," said Mrs. Miller.

Richard reached out for the rope.

It started to move a little.

He closed his eyes.

"Open your eyes," said Mrs. Miller. "And look where you're going."

Richard jumped up a little.

He grabbed the first knot.

"Don't let your feet drag down like that," Mrs. Miller said. "Get them up off the floor."

Richard pulled his feet up under him. He looked at Mrs. Miller.

"I'm right here," she said. "If you fall, you'll fall on me. I'm a great pillow."

Richard reached for the next knot.

He pulled himself up.

He looked down. His feet were even with Mrs. Miller's head.

"Look where you're going, Animal," said Mrs. Miller. "Not where you've been. Just don't kick me in the head."

Richard reached the fourth knot. Then the fifth.

He looked up toward the ceiling.

There was still a long way to go.

"Don't look down," said Mrs. Miller.

Richard took a quick peek.

He was up pretty high.

Very high.

His hands were wet.

"You're doing great," said Mrs. Miller. "You're almost halfway up."

Richard stopped to catch his breath. His hands hurt from holding on. "Far enough," he said.

"One more knot," Mrs. Miller said.

Richard reached up. He pulled himself to the next knot.

"I don't think I can get down," he said.

"Of course you can."

He lowered himself down a little.

After a minute it seemed easier.

Easier than going up.

He jumped down the last foot.

"Not bad," said Mrs. Miller.

"Hey," said Richard. "Pretty good."

He smiled at Mrs. Miller.

"Tomorrow morning we'll do it again," said Mrs. Miller. "When Mr. Bell comes back, you'll have to do it alone."

Richard stopped smiling.

He'd never be able to do it alone.

Never.

"Time to go," said Mrs. Miller.

"Right," said Richard. "Thanks."

He went down the hall.

He couldn't believe he had gone halfway.

Then he sighed.

He'd never be able to get up the rest of the way.

Chapter 9

Richard jumped down the back step.

He started for school.

Holly was still in the kitchen.

She was taking a long time.

She hated shredded wheat.

Good for her.

Richard took a deep breath.

This was the first day he was going to school without her.

His mother said he could.

And all because of Mrs. Miller.

Miller the Killer.

Miller the Pillow.

This morning he was going to climb again with her.

A little higher.

By the time Mr. Bell came back he'd be pretty good.

Not the best.

But nobody would say he was a scaredy cat.

He went down the hall to the gym.

Mrs. Miller wasn't there.

Mr. Bell was tossing a basketball into the hoop.

"Where's Mrs. Miller?" Richard asked.

"My cold is better," said Mr. Bell. "Mrs. Miller is in another school."

Richard backed out of the gym.

He couldn't believe it.

Mrs. Miller was gone.

He'd never be able to climb now.

He went to the classroom.

Some of the kids were there already.

Jill Simon was sitting on the edge of her chair. "I'm not taking any chances," she said. "I'm ready to run if I see a cricket."

Richard went back to look at the skink.

The dot of blood was gone.

The skink must be growing a new tail.

Matthew came back to the science table too.

"I think we should name the skink," Richard said. "Something plain. Something regular. Like Charlie."

"How about Pete?" Matthew asked. "The skink has a trick tail just like your Uncle Pete."

Richard leaned over the tank. "Hey, Pete," he said. He darted his tongue in and out.

The skink did too.

"He likes it," Matthew said.

Richard nodded.

He hoped the skink knew he was sorry.

He went back to his seat.

He started to work on a Mother's Day card.

He made some flowers on the front.

He put a skink in one corner.

A skink with a little tail.

On the back he wrote:

DEAR MOM,

     I'M GLAD YOU LET ME GO TO SCHOOL ALOAN.

     I'M GLAD YOU'RE NOT AFRAD ANY MOOR.

     HAPPY MOTHER DAY.

          LOVE,

          RICHARD BEST

He put his pencil down.

He wished he wasn't afraid.

He wished Mrs. Miller was back.

Just then Mr. Mancina came to the door. "I'm here to see the skink," he said.

"You just caught us," said Ms. Rooney. "It's time for gym."

Mr. Mancina went back to the science table. "He looks great. But where's his tail?"

"Skinks lose their tails sometimes," Richard said. "Mrs. Miller said they grow back."

"Yes," said Ms. Rooney. "Then we read about it in a lizard book."

"There was a picture," said Matthew. "Another lizard grabbed the skink's tail."

"The skink pulled away," said Emily. "He left his tail."

Matthew laughed. "I guess the other lizard thought the skink was still there. He was fighting with an empty tail."

Mr. Mancina smiled. "Mrs. Miller must have been thinking about the skink. She called on the phone. She said to go to see the animal in

Ms. Rooney's room. She said to say he can do it."

"Do what?" asked Ms. Rooney.

Mr. Mancina raised his shoulders in the air. "Grow a tail maybe."

Richard thought about Mrs. Miller.

Maybe she wasn't so bad after all.

Mrs. Miller was thinking about him too.

He bent down. He tied his sneaker laces.

Then he got in line.

The class went down the hall to the gym.

Mr. Bell was waiting for them.

"Climbing day," said Emily.

"Right," said Mr. Bell. "Who'll be first?"

"I can do it," Richard told himself.

"Are you talking to yourself?" Emily asked.

"A little," Richard said.

"Who can do it?" Mr. Bell asked.

"Richard can," said Emily.

"I think Richard's afraid," Jason said.

"Me too," said Timothy.

"I am a little," said Richard. "But everyone's afraid. You're afraid of the skink."

"He's right," Jason told Timothy.

"I'm afraid of the crickets," said Jill.

Richard went to the rope. "Halfway," he told Mr. Bell.

"Good start," said Mr. Bell.

Richard grabbed the rope. It felt rough against his hands.

He thought about Mrs. Miller.

He thought about the skink.

He darted his tongue in and out.

Then he began to climb.